1

When I look back on it now, I realize the day my world fell apart was the best thing that ever happened to me. I found the love of my life, the career of my dreams, and my future is brighter than ever.

It all started on a sunny, Monday morning in the middle of April. I had a great workout at the gym, popped home for a quick shower and breakfast, and headed to my job selling funeral supplies over the phone. It wasn't the most glamorous job in the world, but with the salary and commission, I was making serious money for the first time in my life. Things seemed like they were on an upward trajectory with no ceiling on how far I could go.

I grabbed a cup of coffee in the break room and headed to my desk to go over the day's agenda. There were lots of calls to make, and I liked to get there before everyone else so I could be ready to sell while everyone else was still making the morning adjustment to office life. It didn't hurt that the funeral directors tend to be in the office earlier than most folks, but their secretaries came in around 9:00 am. That meant no gatekeeper to keep me from talking to the decision maker and that meant I made more sales. My cost of living was high because my wife was one that would be considered "high maintenance" by anyone who made less than Bill Gates. I didn't mind it though. She was beautiful, feminine, friendly, and great in the sack. A perfect ten. At least, that's what I thought at the time.

It was unusual to see my boss in his office so early on a Monday, but I shrugged it off and sat down at my desk. I was pulling up my calendar when he came over to talk.

"Good morning, Ryan. I'm glad you came in early. I wanted to talk to you before everyone else came in. Let's go to my office."

I got up, curious as to what this was all about, but excited because I had landed a huge account on Friday. It would make the company millions in profits, and that meant hundreds of thousands in commissions for me. Maybe I was going to get a bonus for all the hard work I've been putting in lately!

"Ryan, do you drink?" he asked, while placing a bottle of Macallan's Sherry Oak 18 on his desk.

Yes! A glass of great Scotch at 8:00 am on a Monday? I'm getting paid!

"I do, sir, but not usually this early in the day. I just had my orange juice about an hour ago," I chuckled.

"Well, make an exception. I have a feeling this is going to be a day with lots of drinks. In fact, this entire bottle is for you."

"Seriously? Thank you! I've always wanted to try this but couldn't bring myself to spend the money on myself," I laughed before continuing, "Are you sure about the bottle, sir? I know Mcallan's isn't cheap."

"It's the least I can do."

After opening the bottle, he pulled out two crystal glasses and poured two fingers in each. He handed one to me then leaned back in his overstuffed, leather office chair. I savored the scent and the color, before taking a sip. It was better than I ever imagined it could be. Maybe I could splurge and buy another bottle or two for myself with the bonus I was surely about to receive.

"Ryan," he began, "You are, without a doubt, the

best salesperson I've ever known. You've made this company a fortune and done pretty well for yourself and your beautiful wife in the process. Wouldn't you agree?"

"Well, I don't know if I'm the best, but I'd agree that this career has enabled me to live a better life than I ever thought I would. Thank you for giving me a shot." I said, blushing at the compliment.

"Don't thank me. I've got some bad news to give you," he said, averting his eyes. He seemed almost ashamed. *What the hell was going on?*

"The owners of the company have decided to shut down the office and outsource all of the sales and marketing to an overseas call center. They've crunched the numbers and figured that even though we'll lose a few customers, the money they'll save on salaries and commission will make up for it. I just found out about this yesterday. I'm being let go as well."

I sat there, stunned. There was a sick feeling in the pit of my stomach, and the scotch seemed to be making it worse. Passing out seemed like an inevitability, but I held on to the arms of the chair and sat there with my mouth agape in silence.

"I… Wait…. Are you joking? I just closed the biggest account in the company's history. They're going to make millions off of this account alone! Now they're just going to pull the rug out from under me, I mean us?" I somehow managed to ask without yelling, cursing, or throwing the glass at the window.

"I think they're making a mistake, but they're greedy bastards. I did manage to convince them to pay you the commission on the initial sale as your severance. Your health and dental insurance will continue for six months as well. I have a check for you in the amount of $300,000. It's only a fraction of what you would have made, but it's the best I could get out of them. I'm sorrier than you could ever know," he said before continuing, "If you want to grab your personal stuff and leave before everyone else gets here, I understand. It's going to be a rough day when this shit hits the proverbial fan."

I thanked him and walked to my desk to begin gathering my possessions. There wasn't much there, but I had some pictures of my wife and family that I wanted to take, along with my briefcase and laptop. The walk to my car seemed like it was in slow motion. Everything seemed so unreal. I just wanted to go home and talk to my wife before she headed off to her job at the gym, hoping that she'd take the day off and commiserate with me. As I pulled out of the parking lot, I saw some of my coworkers pulling in. They had no idea what was coming, so I hastened my departure.

2

Without even remembering the drive, or paying much attention, I pulled into my driveway and headed inside. I stepped in the front door and deactivated the alarm before calling out, "Honey?"

I was greeted with silence. *Did she go to work early too? That's not like her.*

I headed upstairs to our bedroom and started to change clothes. If I was going to be home all day, I was going to be in sweats and slippers and not in the suit I was wearing now. While unbuttoning my shirt, I looked around and noticed some pictures were missing. The one I noticed first was an 8x10 photo of her parents, taken while they were having their second honeymoon in Crete. I noticed others missing as well, but I didn't think much of it. She was always redecorating and moving things around. Decorating was her domain, and I had to admit, she had an eye for style and our bank account balance reflected it. It was worth it, I thought, because a happy wife leads to a happy life, or so I'd been told.

Now wearing sweats and slippers, I headed back downstairs to the kitchen. While I had no intention of drinking the day away as my former boss had suggested, I did feel like drowning my sorrows in a pint of Ben & Jerry's Phish Food while watching some mindless action movies. It was still morning, but without a job I had to be at it really didn't matter. Calories be damned! I was going to treat myself.

When I went to open the freezer door, I noticed the envelope with my name on it. It was in my wife's flowery handwriting, and I was expecting a little love note or poem. She had a habit of leaving them around for me, and I loved it. I opened the envelope with the expectation of a declaration of love and some buoyed spirits. Unfortunately, life had other plans.

"My dear Ryan,

I care so much about you, and this is the hardest thing I've ever had to write, but I have to be honest. I've fallen in love with someone else. Dylan, who owns the gym, and I have been having an affair. I never meant for it to happen, but it started by accident. I'll spare you the details, but we are in love. I never meant to hurt you, but I need to be with Dylan. I love you dearly, but you'll always be more of a friend than a lover to me. We don't have

For the second time of the day, I stood in silence, my mouth agape, and too stunned to think. How could she do this to me? Even after this, I still couldn't bring myself to call her a bitch, even if it was just in my mind. Had I angered the gods somehow? I couldn't think straight, but I picked up my cell and dialed her phone. I needed to hear her explain this. The words needed to come out of her mouth so I would know it was real. Picking up my cell phone, I hit send. She was the last person I had called so it redialed her number.

"I'm sorry, but the number you are trying to reach has been disconnected or is not in service."

That fucking bitch. On second thought, screw Ben & Jerry's. It was going to be a scotch day after all.

3

I woke up on the sofa the next morning with a head
that felt like it was going to explode, and a stomach
on fire from too much booze. Somehow, I managed
to make it to the kitchen where I grabbed a
Gatorade, a Red Bull, and a handful of ibuprofens.
Swallowing the ibuprofen while slamming back the
energy drink, I realized I needed to eat something.
I'd gone the whole day before without eating, but I
managed to finish the bottle of scotch and a couple
of beers too. The thought of food turned my
stomach, but I figured I could keep some saltines
down. I grabbed a sleeve of the crackers, picked up
my Gatorade, and filled a plastic bag with some ice
for my head, before heading upstairs to lay in bed
and recover.

It was about 1:00 pm when I woke up. The
headache had been reduced to a dull throb, and my
stomach didn't feel like a war zone anymore. I
jumped in the shower and turned the water on as
hot as I could stand it, and just stood there until the
water ran cold. After brushing my teeth and getting
dressed, I made my way downstairs, once again
feeling like a human. A sad, confused human, but a
human, nonetheless. Without knowing what my

next steps should be, I went to the phone to call Ginger's parents but thought better of it and hung up. I called my friend, Larry, instead. Larry was a successful attorney who ran a general solo practice out of his home. He'd helped with a couple of real estate issues in the past and I knew he'd be able to give me some solid advice. He answered on the first ring.

"What's up, you magnificent bastard?" he asked, playfully. "Are you ready to let me beat you at a round of golf again, or maybe you'd rather me slaughter you on the tennis court?"

I chuckled lightly. "Well, I've got plenty of time for it now. The company downsized me yesterday. I'm out of work."

"Shit, man… I'm sorry to hear that. What happened?"

After explaining the job loss I told him that wasn't what I was calling about. "Ginger left me for the owner of the gym where she works. I found out yesterday right after getting canned. She left a Dear John on the fridge and disconnected her cell phone. She wants a quick divorce with no alimony or sharing of the assets."

Larry was silent. He and his wife were close friends of ours, and he couldn't believe what I had just told him.

"Dude, I feel like I just said this a minute ago, but I'm sorry. Did you have any idea this was coming? Were you having problems?"

"Not a clue. Just a couple nights ago we were talking about what we would name our kids when the time came. The hits just kept coming yesterday I'm recovering from the world's worst hangover right now."

Larry and his wife came over that night and brough dinner. While gorging ourselves on Chinese takeout, we discussed what my next steps should be. He explained that he could file for a quick divorce, and that we would be officially single again in about six months. I told him to get the process started. I just wanted it over and done.

4

The next six months went by quickly. Emotionally, I felt dead inside, but outwardly I was doing great. After joining a different gym in the next town, I started working out like a fiend. I was able to pack on twenty pounds of muscle and get even more lean than I already was. I put the house on the market and got about 30% more for it than what I had put into it. That, along with the $300k severance had given me a nice nest egg to go along with the money I already had in savings. There was no rush to find a job, but I knew I'd need to find something before my insurance went away. The problem is that I had no idea what I wanted to do. While working out one day, I bumped into an old friend of mine from my college days, Rich. We had worked together at a jewelry store inside a mall. It was a large chain, and I enjoyed the job, but it wasn't a career. At least, I didn't think it was for me. He was still there, but now he was a regional manager.

"You ever thought about selling jewelry again?" he asked while we were getting dressed in the locker room.

"Not really. It was a fun job, and it paid my way through college, but I never really saw it as a career for myself," I replied. "It seems to have worked out well for you though. I saw the BMW you drove in before I realized who you were."

"Ryan, it's great. Don't get me wrong though. It's a lot of work, and I often feel like a babysitter to my store managers and their staff, but the money is great, and my wife loves the discounts. She's drowning in diamonds."

"That's awesome, man. I remember making okay money selling jewelry during college, but I guess that management does make a lot more than the salespeople."

"We do, and I need an assistant manager at the store here across the river. I've interviewed a bunch of people, but everyone is so lazy now. They want to make bank while doing nothing but posting pics on Instagram. I need an adult who will help whip the store into shape. I just put a new general manager in there last week, and she needs an assistant. It doesn't pay what you're used to and it's a bit of a drive, but the benefits are solid, and the money is decent with some monthly bonuses that really make it worthwhile."

"You sure you're not still in sales and trying to close me?" I jokingly asked him.

"Once a salesperson, always a salesperson. I'll tell you what, let me buy you a steak dinner tonight and we can talk about it some more."

Never one to turn down a free meal, I accepted his invitation. We spent the evening discussing the job, interspersed with plenty of reminiscing about college. It was a good time, and before I jumped into an Uber to ride home, I had accepted his offer on the condition that I didn't know how long I would stay. He understood, and we made plans to meet the next afternoon to fill out the new hire paperwork. My start date was the following Monday.

5

The weekend came and went, and I showed up Monday morning to the new job. The commute was longer than I expected, taking about 45 minutes in traffic. I didn't like that, but I still had a good attitude and was excited to be getting back to being a productive member of society. Keeping with my usual habit of being early getting to work, I arrived about a half hour before I was supposed to be there. The mall wasn't officially open yet, but there were plenty of senior citizen mall walkers as well as employees coming in and out. I hadn't met anyone that I'd be working with yet, so I just parked myself on a bench outside the shop and waited until someone else showed up to unlock the doors.

I'll admit I was enjoying the scenery while I waited. had forgotten how many cuties worked at malls, and some of them were absolutely smoking hot. Sadly, with me being 34, a lot of them were way too young for me, but it was enjoyable just seeing who else was out there. I hadn't dated since Ginger left me, but I was starting to feel a lot better about myself. Maybe I'd meet someone here at work that I could enjoy spending time with. Hopefully, they'd be a little closer to my own age group.

I just happened to be looking at the door to the mal

when Kenna walked in. I didn't know who she was, but I had to roll my tongue up and put it back in my mouth before she noticed me gawking. She was gorgeous. She was tall for a woman and had long jet-black hair and blue eyes the color of crystals. Long-legged, curvy, with full, pouty lips just made her the perfect package. She made her way to the store and started to unlock the roll-down gate. *Did she work there too?* This job was already proving to be better than I thought!

Grabbing my bag, I approached the store. She noticed me and turned my way, delaying opening the gate while determining whether I was a shady character.

"Are you Kenna, by any chance?" I asked.

"I am," she replied. "You must be Ryan?"

"Reporting for duty," snapping off a goofy salute.

Did I just do that? What the hell is wrong with me? I've seen beautiful women before. Chill, dude, chill.

Kenna just laughed, and commented on my eagerness, but I still felt like an idiot.

We rolled up the gate and walked into the store

together, then shut the gate behind us. She showed me around, and then we began the process of opening the store. Sheets needed to be pulled off the display cases. Diamonds needed to be taken from the safe and placed on display, and the register needed to be set up. As we worked, she showed me where everything went and gave a quick tutorial on the register.

"It's just you and me here today until noon, then the shift supervisor comes in. She'll close the store tonight, and you and I are out of here at 6, unless we're busy." Kenna said. Her voice was a little husky, and everything she said sounded sultry. I felt a stirring in my pants when she bent over to lift the gate.

Dude… Get it together! You don't want to be pitching a tent when your new boss turns around.

"If you don't have plans, I was hoping we could grab coffee or dinner after we get off so we could get to know each other. I have specific goals I want to achieve here, and I want to make sure we're sympatico. The last managers really let this place go, so we've got our work cut out for us."

"I totally understand. I'm free, and I'd prefer to grab dinner if that's okay. I don't like to eat a big meal after 8:00. I've got to maintain my girlish figure," I joked.

Kenna laughed out loud before saying, "You don't even know. The struggle is real."

We grabbed dinner at a local chain restaurant. We both ordered drinks while waiting for our meals to arrive. The conversation started off in a personal direction. I gave Kenna a brief rundown of the day from hell and rebooting my life. She expressed sympathy without being condescending and told me she hadn't dated in years.

"I find that hard to believe. Without meaning to sound inappropriate, you're extremely attractive, you have a good job, and so far, I'd have to say you have a great personality. You must have guys asking you out all the time."

Kenna blushed. "Thank you, Ryan. That's nice to hear, and you handled it well. It's not that I don't get asked out. I just haven't met a guy that I really want to share myself with."

"I can dig that," I dropped the subject.

Our meals came, and the food was good. We ended up having another round of drinks and just chatted for about an hour after we ate. Once we realized we were on the same page regarding our management styles, the conversation became light and we laughed and spoke freely. We really hit it off well and I ended up having a great time.

6

A couple months went by, and I quickly realized I enjoyed working at the jewelry store. We had weeded out any problem employees, and the store was performing better than ever. Kenna and I became close friends and had dinner together a couple times a week. While it wasn't a romantic thing, it was still nice to spend time together. I was still strongly attracted to her, and I got the impression that something might be there, but I didn't want to press the issue and take a chance on messing up my job or our friendship.

While at work one Monday, Kenna approached me to discuss an upcoming sale we were having that coming Friday.

"We're having the diamond show sale this weekend. Normally it would just be a one-day thing, but they're extending it through the entire weekend. I'll need you here open to close on Friday, Saturday, and Sunday." she said. "I'm sorry, but I'll be here too. So much for a fun-filled weekend."

"Not a problem. As usual, I don't have plans. Getting up super-early to make the commute after getting home late is going to suck, but it's only a couple days. Maybe I'll get a hotel room on this side of the water, so I don't have to deal with it."

Kenna paused. "I have an idea. Feel free to say no if it would be weird, but I've got a spare room in my apartment. You'd have your own bathroom, and it's got a queen-sized bed with a brand-new mattress. I've never even taken the plastic cover off. You're welcome to stay with me for the weekend, if you're cool with spending that much time with your old boss."

"You old? You look like you're 25. You're anything but old. If you're sure it wouldn't be too much trouble, I'd love to take you up on the offer."

"Awesome! It'll be like a slumber party! Bring your goofiest pajamas! By the way, I appreciate the compliment, but I'm 30."

"Well, you sure don't look it."

I was excited about spending the nights at Kenna's house. Scenarios of how we might end up in the same bed kept running through my mind all day, and it was a struggle to conceal my partial erection. When I got home that night, I dreamt about Kenna in every possible sexual situation. My mind was racing with thoughts of how gorgeous her breasts were once her blouse was off and her bra was on the floor. Picturing myself licking and sucking her dark nipples, before working my way down between her legs and tasting her wetness. My alarm went off right as I was getting ready to enter her with my rock-hard cock. I woke up sweating with an erection that looked like it was going to split the skin on my penis.

Wow… I knew my attraction to her was strong, but damn… I want to make love to her so badly that I'm about to burst. I want to breed her and spend the rest of my life waking up next to her.

The rest of the week seemed to crawl by, but it seemed like Kenna was being flirtier than normal. Was it possible that she was into me too? I hoped so, but I didn't want to jinx it.

7

Friday morning finally arrived, and we both got to the store about an hour before we were set to open. Kenna was perfection in a little black dress that accentuated her every curve. She had to know that she was driving any guy might see her crazy. I couldn't help but have an erection. My penis was straining against my pants, and I knew I had to get myself under control before we opened the doors.

While putting a tray of diamond earrings in the display case at the front of the store, Kenna accidentally backed into me when she stood up. Her perfect ass brushed right against my raging erection, and I swear she lingered for a second before blushing and walking back to the safe. Had she stayed there a second longer, I would've soaked the front of my slacks with the cum I wanted to put into her. I knew she felt my manhood when she did that and I wasn't sure how to handle the situation. When Kenna came out of the back room, she gave me an impish grin. The game was on.

It was insanely busy that day. We had record sales and neither of us had time to dwell on what had happened that morning. As we were closing, I suggested that I would stop and grab some takeout for dinner on my way back to her place. She agreed, before adding, "Hurry home though."

When I arrived, she was already dressed in pajamas. They weren't risqué, just a white tank top with pink bottoms covered in cartoon bunnies. Somehow, the innocence of the outfit made her even sexier. I changed into my lounge pants and a t-shirt, and we proceeded to lay waste to the dinner I had picked up. After we ate, we talked for a few minutes before deciding to hit the sack. As we each made way to our bedrooms, Kenna stopped and reached over to touch my hand.

"I just want you to know that I appreciate you. You're so good to me, and you've never acted the least bit inappropriately towards me even though I know you feel the same attraction that I do. You treat me like a lady, and I just want to thank you for that."

"Kenna, I would never disrespect you. You ARE a lady, and I will always treat you that way. You're right. I am attracted to you. You're beautiful, funny, smart, and incredibly sexy. I'm crazy about you, but you're also my best friend. If that's all we ever are, I can live with that, but you'll always have my respect and love."

Kenna pulled me in for an embrace and laid her head on my shoulder. Her hair smelled amazing, like the fruit scented shampoo and conditioner she used. Her perfume was mostly worn off after such a long day, but just a hint of the muskiness remained. I turned my hips to the side to avoid impaling her with my erection and held her. I loved her. I already knew I loved her, but in that moment, the emotion overwhelmed me, and I knew I just wanted to spend my life taking care of this incredible woman.

As she pulled away, she paused to look into my

eyes. Her eyes were so blue, and they pierced me as she looked into mine. She leaned forward slightly and kissed me lightly on the corner of my mouth before saying, "thank you." She turned and walked into her bedroom, closing the door behind her. I stood there for a few minutes, still stunned by the last few moments. Eventually, I shook it off and fell into a deep, dreamless sleep.

Saturday morning, we got up and shared coffee and bagels before getting dressed and ready for the long day ahead. Sure enough, it was another record-breaking day. As we were closing the store, Kenna told me she had given our third-key assistant the next day off in exchange for working a double on Monday. That would give her and me a day off to recover before coming back on Tuesday. I wasn't complaining a bit.

Once again, we grabbed some takeout and headed back to her place. We both changed into our sleepwear and shared a large pepperoni pizza and a six-pack of beer in front of the television. She leaned over and put her head on my shoulder and pulled my arm around her. It felt like we had always been together. We woke up the next morning in the same position. I could get used to this.

8

When we woke up Sunday, I started to pack my bag and strip off the bed clothes. I had really enjoyed staying here and I hated to go, but the sale was over today. We closed early on Sundays at around 5:00 pm, so I would head straight home from work. I set my bag by the door and went in the kitchen and found Kenna putting cream cheese on a couple of bagels and pouring two cups of coffee.

"What's with the bag?"

"Well, since today is the last day of the sale and we're off tomorrow, I figured I'd give you your space back. I'm sure you're ready to get back to your swinging single ways."

"Ryan, I've really enjoyed having you here the last couple of days. It's been nice to have someone to talk to at night. Normally, I'm by myself. I don't go out a lot, so it gets a bit lonely sometimes. I was kind of hoping you'd stay one more night. We could go out to dinner after we close, and maybe we could hang out and do something tomorrow since we're both off. I'll buy dinner. You paid for our food the last two nights. What do you say? Can I buy you dinner?"

"I'm never one to turn down a free meal, and I can't imagine anyone I'd rather eat with than you. I'm up for it as long as you aren't sick of me."

"Never. Now, hurry up. I ordered an Uber to take us to work today so we could have some wine with dinner tonight without worrying about driving."

Sunday was as busy as the previous two days. Even though it was a short day, it seemed like it was taking forever. I was so excited about being able to spend some time with Kenna without feeling rushed or exhausted, but it seemed like the day just wasn't going to end. Finally, it did. We caught another Uber to the restaurant and shared a wonderful dinner and a couple bottles of ice-cold Pinot Grigio.

"Have you dated at all since you and your wife split up?" Kenna asked while pouring two more glasses of wine.

"No. Not at all. Some of my friends tried to set me up a few times, and one even tricked me into what was supposed to be a blind date. That turned out to be a hilarious disaster. After that, I just kind of gave up. I figured I'd know when I was ready to date again. No rush."

"How close are you to feeling ready? I'm just wondering. Forgive me if I'm being too nosy. This wine makes me chatty," she giggled.

"I think I'm ready. Why? Do you know anyone?" We both laughed and finished the wine and ordered another Uber. She leaned against me all the way back to her apartment. Her bare leg was pressed up against my slacks, and I found myself aroused to the point of being lightheaded.

When we got back up to her apartment, I couldn't hold back any longer. I pulled Kenna into an embrace and moved in for a kiss. It was now or never. I couldn't hide my disappointment when she turned her head and said, "Wait… We need to talk."

"Kenna, I love you. I want to spend the rest of my life with you. I've known you were special from the first moment I laid eyes on you, and I think I started falling in love as soon as we met. If you don't feel the same way, just tell me now. Go ahead and get it over with so I can try to move on," I said, my voice trembling with passion, rage, or frustration. Maybe all three.

"I know, Ryan. I love you too, and I want to spend the rest of my life with you as well. There are just some things you don't know about me that I need to tell you. You need to know what you're getting into before doing something you can't undo. Okay?"

"Okay. I don't care what it is, Kenna. I just want you. What is it that I need to know?"

Kenna led me over to the sofa, and we sat down, facing each other. Kenna started to talk, but finally just said, "It might be easier if I just show you, but I don't want you to get angry or think I tried to deceive you."

"I won't. What do you want to show me?"

"Before we get into that, let's both get changed for bed. You're not in any shape to drive home right now, so you're staying either way. Okay?"

"Alright. I'll meet you back out here in a few minutes," I said while getting up and heading towards the bedroom. I was starting to get frustrated. Not only was my cock engorged to the point of no return, but my emotions were rubbed raw from what seemed like a game she was playing. What the hell did she want to tell me? Rather, what did she want to show me?

After changing into a comfortable pair of shorts and an old tee, I came back out and sat on the couch. I still had a raging erection, but my temper had settled a bit. I had realized that whatever it was that she was trying to tell me was obviously something that was difficult for her. By getting angry, I wasn't being much of a friend. I loved this woman, and if I wanted to spend the rest of my life with her, patience was going to be important.

A few minutes later, Kenna appeared in the living room wearing a kimono and looking sexier than ever. We just looked at each other without saying a word for several minutes before she spoke first.

"I've never shared this part of myself with any man before. I hope this doesn't ruin things between us, but you're the man I want to share my life with so here goes." she said, while untying the bow on her kimono and letting it drop to the floor.

9

Once again, I found myself stunned and speechless. Before me stood the most beautiful, perfect specimen of a woman that I had ever seen. Her breasts were perfect, and just as I had imagined them, down to the cinnamon tinted nipples that were hardened with arousal. Her tummy was flat, accented by a diamond dangling from her navel ring. Her skin was flawless and tanned, and looked delicious. Between her legs was the surprise I had been waiting for. An eight-inch, engorged cock pointed at me, the head purple with excitement. My mind, my heart, my manhood swirled with confusion as Kenna stood there with a shy look on her face, seeking my approval.

I did the only thing I could do. Standing up from the couch, I walked over to Kenna and reached for her chin. She flinched, thinking I was going to smack her, but I tilted her face up towards mine and I kissed her more deeply than I have ever kissed anyone before. She wrapped her arms around me and kissed me back hungrily, as her cock bounced against mine. We devoured each other's mouths, our tongues entwined to the point where it was impossible to tell where hers began and mine ended. We pulled our lips apart and she leaned her head back, allowing me to nibble, suck, and caress her neck with my tongue and teeth. She moaned gutturally, and it drove me wild. When I pulled myself away and looked at her face, she was crying.

"Kenna, baby, what's wrong? Why are you crying? I'm not mad. I swear I'm not. Can't you tell?" I pleaded while trying to kiss away every tear.

"It's not that. I just… I thought for sure you would reject me when you saw what I was. I was so scared of losing you because I've fallen so head over heels in love with you. You don't hate me? You're not mad that I'm not all female?" she asked me, while holding onto me like I was going to float away if she let go.

"No, no, no… I was surprised, of course. This isn't something I expected, but Kenna, I fell in love with you when your clothes were on. I didn't fall in love with your genitals. While this wasn't what I was expecting to find underneath your clothes, I must admit that it's exciting. I love you, and you are ALL female. You are a lady… You're my lady, if you'll have me."

"I'm yours, Ryan. All of me is yours." she said, then took my hand and led me into her bedroom.

10

Kenna led me to her bed, and slowly undressed me, kissing every spot she uncovered. I picked her up and laid her on the bed gently, before laying down and kissing her neck. Our mouths met again and we kissed deeply, wetly, and passionately. I slowly started to move down her body to her breasts, inhaling her right nipple and nibbling it lightly as she gasped and gripped my head. I found myself wanting to taste every inch of her, working my lips and tongue over her tummy, navel, and finding myself transfixed by her throbbing cock.

"I've never done this before. I hope I'm not horrible at it," I said before licking the underside of her pen and planting wet kisses around the purple head.

"You don't have to do that if you aren't ready. I understand it's a lot to take in, no pun intended," she giggled.

"Oh, don't worry about that. I want to. I want to please you," I said, while stroking her cock with both hands. I spat on her cock and moved my lips around the head, and up and down the shaft. She moaned, and I opened my mouth, swallowing her member while massaging it with the roughest parts of my tongue, just like I'd seen my favorite porn stars do on Pornhub. I never thought I'd be the one giving the blowjob, but my life had proven itself to be full of surprises recently. I worked my way up and down her rod while Kenna writhed and moaned. In a moment of excitement, she grabbed the back of my head and pushed down a little too hard. I gagged, and pulled my mouth off her cock, but kept slowly stroking it.

"Easy, girl… Remember that I'm new at this. I'll get it all down my throat, but it's going to take some practice," I teased.

Kenna laughed and apologized, before giving me some advice. "Open your mouth and let my cock slide back on your tongue. When you feel like you're about to gag, swallow hard and you can go all the way down."

I continued to tease her dick with my tongue, sliding it in and out of my mouth, then stopping when it seemed like she was getting close to coming. I was edging her, and I wasn't going to stop until she had reached her absolute peak. I worked my way back up her shaft before easing her cock back between my lips. As I slowly worked my mouth and tongue further down her pulsating phallus, I felt the instinctive gag, but I doubled down and swallowed hard. Without a hitch, I found myself with the entire length of her penis buried in my throat and my tongue softly teasing her balls. Working my way back and forth, up and down, alternating between slow strokes with my tongue, and fast, furious motion, I felt Kenna's balls tighten.

"Oh my god! I'm going to come. Pull it out!" I wouldn't relent. I continued to massage her cock with my lips and tongue and within seconds her cock began to pulsate in my mouth. Before I knew it, my mouth was filled with Kenna's seed. I couldn swallow it fast enough and it ran down the corners of my lips. I was surprised to find that the taste was pleasant. Salty, thick, and almost creamy, I rolled i around in my mouth, savoring it before swallowing it in one massive gulp. Kenna was panting and looked like she was in another dimension. I ran my fingers around my mouth and licked off every drop of spunk that was still on my face, before cleaning the rest from Kenna's balls and tummy.

I slowly kissed my way up her body, until I reached her neck, then asked, "So, how'd I do? I realize it's my first time, but I promise I'll get better. I'm a fast learner, particularly when I like what I'm learning."

Kenna exhaled and sighed, "Are you sure that was your first time? If it had been any better, I may hav had a stroke! You didn't have to let me come in your mouth though. I'm sure that wasn't something you really wanted to do, but it was hella hot."

"Believe it or not, I wanted you to come in my mouth. I've fantasized about tasting you, and even though this wasn't what I was thinking of, I loved it. You taste great, and now you have me wondering if I should've been sucking cocks my whole life!"

We both giggled and kissed. As our kisses slowly became more and more passionate, Kenna took hold of my rigid erection. I almost came all over her hand right then, but she gripped it firmly before saying, "My turn!"

Kenna's mouth was like Disneyland for my penis. She kissed my cock, licked it hungrily, before spitting on it and stroking the entire length. She looked into my eyes as she pleasured me, then stopped altogether and said, "I'm ready for you to fuck me, Daddy."

I rolled her over on her stomach, and she stuck her perfect, round apple bottom in the air and spread her cheeks apart with her hands. Without a second thought, I buried my face in her ass and started licking and sucking her hole. She moaned in ecstasy, and I worked up a big ball of spit and let it dribble into her asshole while sliding my finger in slowly.

"Oh god… please fuck me. PUT YOUR COCK IN ME!!! PLEASE!!!"

Obligingly, I got up on my knees and slowly pressed the head of my penis into her tiny little asshole. It didn't seem like it was going to fit, but once the head moved past her sphincter, her ass gripped me like it was custom made for my cock. Kenna groaned, and I began to work my cock back and forth in her ass, slowly building up speed and intensity. No pussy had ever held my dick like this, and I was going to make this last as long as possible.

Kenna was grunting like an animal, while slamming her ass up against my groin repeatedly. It was taking everything I had to keep from exploding in her ass. She slammed against my ass one final time before pulling my dick out and flopping over on her back.

"I want to see you while you fuck me," she growled before throwing her legs over my shoulder and pulling my cock back inside of her. Fucking her like that while looking at her blue eyes and perfect face made me realize that this was what I had been looking for all my life. She was here and I was inside of her.

Kenna slid her legs down to my side and wrapped them around my hips. I leaned forward and fucked her slowly, taking long strokes in and out of her ass, while kissing her. This was heaven.

"Oh shit, I'm going to come again!" Kenna cried out.

"Me too, but how are you going to come? I'm not touching your cock." I asked, while furiously pumping her with every ounce of strength I had.

"My prostate… Don't worry about it! JUST DON'T STOP FUCKING ME!!!" she screamed.

My balls tightened, and Kenna began to moan loudly. Her ass pulsated around my cock as she arched her back and let out a cry of passion. Her beautiful cock began to pulsate and shot thick, creamy ropes of cum all over her flat tummy. The sight of this was too much for me and I let loose, exploding into her ass and coming for what seemed like an eternity. I collapsed onto her with my cock still inside of her. I began to work my way down her stomach, cleaning up every bit of the mess she had made while climaxing. I couldn't get enough of this girl's cum!

We laid in each other's arms, wrapped together like branches twisted together by a windstorm. We spent the rest of that night and all-day Monday making love. When I asked Kenna if she wanted to fuck me with that beautiful cock of hers, she explained to me that she was a "bottom." She wanted me to be the dominant one in the bedroom but maybe on a special occasion she might fuck me if I really wanted her to. I'm really looking forward to the next special occasion.

11

The next morning, I called Rich and turned in my resignation. He was puzzled as to why I was leaving so soon after starting, particularly considering the success we'd been having at the store. When I explained that Kenna and I had fallen in love, he understood and wished me well. Before my last day, I bought Kenna a beautiful two carat flawless diamond with my discount. It was going to be rough not being together all day, every day, but we'd be together every night and that was perfect.

I sold my house and moved in with Kenna. Again, I did well on the sale, coming out well ahead of what I had invested in the house. This led me to consider going into real estate. I did, and I've never been happier. The best part is that I can take time off whenever Kenna is off work so we can spend more time together.

Tomorrow is our one-year anniversary. I've been waiting for a special occasion, and I think Kenna is looking forward to it as well.